D0938441

THIS BOOK IS A GIFT FROM THE FRIENDS OF THE ORINDA LIBRARY

THE
FRIENDS OF THE
ORINDA
LIBRARY

WITHDRAWN

When spring flowers bloom
and grass starts to grow

When we see from the
window a robin or wren

And squirrels play high up in the trees once again...

Passover is on its way.

When everyone scurries
from room to room

With a bucket and mop or a long-handled broom...

Passover is on its way.

When all of the windows and floors start to shine

And our whole house smells clean and looks extra fine...

Passover is on its way.

When our fanciest dishes come out of the drawer
And Elijah's cup sparkles like diamonds galore...

Passover is on its way.

When our house smells of kugel and sweet matzo cake
And cinnamon for the charoset we'll make...

Passover is on its way.

When the sun's getting low and the doorbell stops ringing

And everyone's ready for stories and singing...

When the Seder is ready and candles are lit

And Nana's shown everyone just where to sit...

Passover is here!

31901056307244

Library of Congress Cataloging-in-Publication
data is on file with the publisher.

Text copyright © 2015 by Chris Barash
Pictures by Alessandra Psacharopulo
Published in 2015 by Albert Whitman & Company
ISBN 978-0-8075-6330-4

All rights reserved. No part of this book may be reproduced or transmitted in any
form or by any means, electronic or mechanical, including photocopying,
recording, or by any information storage and retrieval system,
without permission in writing from the publisher.

Printed in China.
10 9 8 7 6 5 4 3 2 NP 20 19 18 17 16 15

Design by Jordan Kost

For more information about Albert Whitman & Company,
visit our web site at www.albertwhitman.com.